To Hibiki and Miki with my love

Published by Picture Book Studio, Saxonville, MA.
Distributed in Canada by Vanwell Publishing, St. Catharines, Ont.

Printed in Hong Kong.
10 9 8 7 6 5 4 3 2 1

Library of Congress Cataloging in Publication Data
Yoshi.
The butterfly hunt / by Yoshi.
Summary: A boy pursues and captures elusive butterflies but decides that it is more fun to carry home his memories than a trophy.
ISBN 0-88708-137-1 : $14.95
[1. Butterflies–Fiction.] I. Title.
PZ7.Y8255Bu 1990
[E]–dc20 90-7361

YOSHI

The Butterfly Hunt

Picture Book Studio

Once there was a boy...

who was surprised by a butterfly.

He wanted to capture the butterfly
and make it his very own.

The boy thought,
"I will do anything to make him mine."

"Anything!"

"I will take him home
and keep him for my pet."

"If I am very quiet…

and very careful...

he will be ***mine!***"

Once there was a boy who was surprised by a butterfly.
He captured the butterfly, and then...

he set it free.

And forever and ever
the butterfly was his very own.